THE UGLY BUG CLUB

Written by Gail Abbitt

Illustrated by Rosie Venner

For Harriet, Tess, Finn, Aracely,
Inez and Dorothy.

First published 2018 by
Ugly Bug Club publishing.

www.theuglybugclub.com

Uniquely **G**ifted **L**oveable **Y**ou!

My name is ....

My favourite bug is ....

At the bottom of the garden, Next to a tree, A snail could be heard saying,

"Oh, it's tough being me!"

"My body is lumpy,
I leave slime where I go,

I'm scared of my shadow
and I'm ever so slow.

Whenever people see m
I'm always ignored,

What I would give to be adored."

A spider was listening
from up in her web,

"You think you have problems,
try being me instead!
When people see me they run
and they scream,

To be ignored
would be a
dream!"

"I try to be friendly and say hello,
But when anyone sees me
away they go!

I'm ever so lonely,
what I would give for a hug.
But nobody loves me;

I'm an
ugly bug!"

A woodlouse overheard the spider and snail,
He opened his mouth and

let out a wail.

"You think you have problems,
you think life is tough?"

He took a deep breath
and let out a huff!

"My body is grey,
my legs are too small,
I've spent my whole life
wanting to be tall."

He looked at the spider
with her legs so long,
And thought to
himself, she has
nothing wrong.

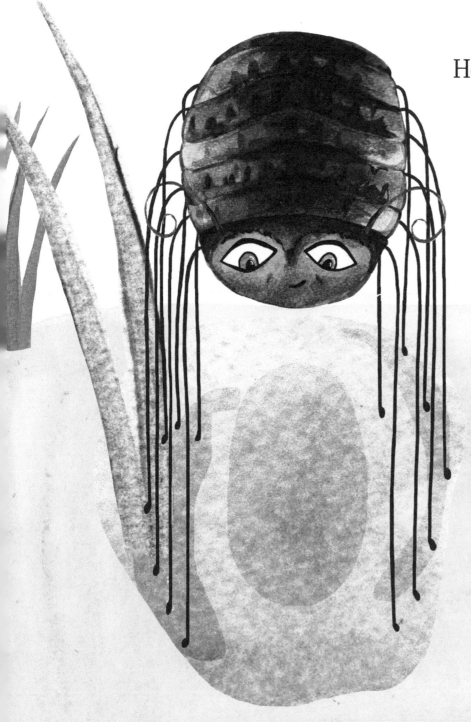

Then he looked at the snail
  and started to moan,
if only I got
    to carry my home!

An insect walked past
and heard all the fuss,

"Hello" he said,
"my name
is Gus.

I couldn't help hearing
what you all had to say,
I would like to join in
if that's okay?"

"Go ahead," said the spider
"it's good to share."

Gus thought to himself,
it's nice that
they care.

"I wish
I was
small
like the woodlouse,"
he cried.

"Or smart
   like a spider,"
he said with a sigh.

"If only my body
was silver

not

brown,

I wouldn't be named after

a stick on

the ground."

From under a cabbage leaf,
Out popped a slug,

"I have an idea

lets start
a club?

We can meet right here and
help each other see,

that all of us are special,"
she said with glee.

"So when we feel sad or when we feel down,
We will always know there's someone around."

Today is the day, right here by this shrub,
for the very first meeting of the

Ugly Bug Club!

Bugs are awesome!

Can you remember when the **snail** says " I'm scared of my shadow and I'm ever so slow." Well this is true, the slow part anyway! The common garden snail is one of the slowest creatures on the Earth!

The **woodlouse** may have been sad that he was short and grey, but woodlice are the only member of the crustacean family (crabs, lobsters etc...) that are able to live on the ground. All other crustaceans spend their life in or near the water.

Spiders are blessed with super 'spidey senses' but their eyesight isn't one of them. They need to rely on the vibrations of the web strands to tell them when they have captured prey, as they struggle to see.

Gus the stick insect may wish that he was small like a woodlouse or smart like a spider, but he can do something that I bet both of them wish they could do! Stick insects can shed and re-grow their limbs to escape predators. How amazing is that!

And last but not least **slugs**! Next time you see a **slug** in the garden, look at the slimey mark it leaves behind. This slime has special chemicals in it that means that the slug will always be able to find their way home.

Lightning Source UK Ltd.
Milton Keynes UK
UKHW051942240620
365454UK00002B/14